Luning-Ning is Lenie Palor's first children's st[illegible]ok and the culmination of reading and telling st[illegible]over twenty years. As a nanny, wor[illegible]hroughout the world, Lenie wo[illegible] children. She has never lost sigh[illegible]ole story can bring.

When bedtime boo[illegible], some children – if still awake – would often wa[illegible] one more story please'. In those brief moments, Lenie would often spontaneously tell a quick story. Lost in that inventive and imaginative world of make believe, adventure and awe, she was inspired to write. During the Covid pandemic and lengthy lockdowns she finally had the time and opportunity.

Lenie was born in the Philippines and has worked, lived and traveled extensively in many parts of the world. She now lives in the UK, is a keen tennis player (and instructor), swims, cooks and still loves telling stories.

Luning-Ning

Written by

Lenie Palor

Illustrations by

Andrew Burroughs

SilverWood

Published in 2022 by SilverWood Books

SilverWood Books Ltd
14 Small Street, Bristol, BS1 1DE, United Kingdom
www.silverwoodbooks.co.uk

ISBN 978-1-80042-217-9 (paperback)

British Library Cataloguing in Publication Data
A CIP catalogue record for this book is
available from the British Library

Page design and typesetting by SilverWood Books

This book is dedicated to Angel

Contents

Introduction

How did I come to write this story? I remember only too well. It was 2020; around Holy Week, which is a long weekend. There was nothing to do because it was the beginning of the Covid pandemic. I could not go anywhere because everywhere was locked down. I was frustrated, anxious, sad and lonely, trying to figure out what to do. I found it really hard because I had always been an outdoor person, and now suddenly I could not go out. My outdoor experiences when I was growing up came to my mind and I started to write down my memories, to relive my childhood.

I never thought that this story would be published, but I sent it to a friend of mine, who thought it was a sweet story; then another friend said the same. Their reactions encouraged me and gave me the idea to write a book. Also, I was reminded of when I worked as a nanny in London about six years ago. I cared for a little boy, and every time I put him to bed, after I had read him three storybooks, he would ask me to make up a story for him. I would tell him these stories, which are based on my memories of growing up in the Philippines.

Reliving these memories gave me a sense of escape during those difficult times of the pandemic. They allowed me to focus my mind on something else. Perhaps I can inspire other aspiring writers to do the same: to tell their stories and show children around the world what it is like to be a child in the Global South-East.

Lenie Palor
2022

1

Luning-Ning Comes to Live with Us

A great-uncle of mine was looking for someone to care for one of his buffalo. He had so many that he could not look after them all, and he was old and needed to scale back his physical labour. He had a huge plot of land and only needed strong male buffalo to do the work, so he was happy to give this female to anyone who wanted her.

One day he approached my father to ask whether he would look after her, and my father said yes immediately. I was thrilled. My father could not afford a buffalo – they cost a fortune – so he was glad to accept my great-uncle's gift. It would help him enormously with his farming work. They agreed to breed her, and that her first calf would belong to my father (which would help him with his farming) and her second calf to my great-uncle. I was excited – this buffalo had given birth already, so my father was hopeful that she would produce another calf.

The buffalo my great-uncle offered my father was his least favourite: a female with a broken right horn. She was six years old when she came to us. I thought he was a good person to be looking out for my father, but my father also helped him a lot with his farming. I didn't ask how her horn had been broken; I was too busy admiring her, though I wondered how it had happened. I thought it must have been awful, and I imagined all sorts of things. Maybe she'd had a fight with another buffalo, or it had got stuck in the branch of a big tree? Maybe she had hit it on a big rock at the river? I told myself I would ask my father and my great-uncle how she had broken it.

One day, early in the morning, the female buffalo was dropped off at our house. My father and I spent time looking at her. She had beautiful, shiny skin that was dark grey in colour, almost black, but she looked a bit sorry for herself. Perhaps she felt sad that my great-uncle had rejected her? She stood quietly and let us walk around her and have a good look at her. She shuffled her feet a few times as I stroked the skin on her back. It was as if she liked it. I continued walking around her, looking into her twinkly eyes. I thought she was lovely.

My great-uncle said goodbye to my father and prepared to leave. Just before he departed, he approached me and asked whether I would help my father to look after the buffalo. Immediately I said yes. I could not explain the extent of my happiness. I jumped for joy.

My great-uncle gave the buffalo a good pat on her back, said goodbye and told her that she was in good hands. She swung her tail from side to side and moved her back feet, almost as if she were dancing. I sensed that she was happy to stay with us for a long time, and I knew I would do anything to help my father look after her. I decided to call her Luning-Ning, which means "sparkly and shiny" in my native language of Ilocano, which is commonly spoken in Gonzaga, a town in the Cagayan Province along the northern tip of Luzon in the Philippines.

After my great-uncle departed, I told my father what he had said and asked if I could help him to look after Luning-Ning. He said yes, absolutely, but he worried that I was only eight years old. Perhaps I was a bit too young? I assured him that I knew how to tie her reins securely to the mango tree. I demonstrated how my great-uncle had tied her up when he'd arrived. Then I undid the reins and tied them a second time, just to prove that I knew what I was doing so that my father would trust me with Luning-Ning. I looked at my father's face to gauge his reaction. He smiled and seemed impressed. I even showed him another way to tie up Luning-Ning, and he told me he trusted me with her. He stressed one important thing: that Luning-Ning was in our care and we must always make sure she was safe and well fed. We had to love and look after her while she was with us.

During that first day, Luning-Ning lay under a mango tree. My father told me that she needed to stay out of the sun around midday as it could reach up to forty degrees Celsius. If exposed to that heat for a long time, she could die. He explained that buffalo should only work for a certain length of time in the sun; then both buffalo and farmer would stop for a rest. If there was a stream or a river nearby, buffalo would normally rest in the water, or just in the shade, being splashed from a bucket.

On that first day, we just let her be herself and get used to us. The mango tree was at the side of our house and we, like Luning-Ning, used it as our resting place during the day. It was huge and gave us a lot of shade. In the middle of the day, I gave her a bucket of water and she lapped it up happily. Afterwards she licked her lips and lay down again in the shade.

Later in the afternoon, when it was time to feed Luning-Ning, my father and I rode on her back to a field where she could eat luscious green grass, which all buffalo like to eat. I sat still behind my father, wrapping my arms around his waist, and asked if I might ride Luning-Ning by myself one day. Patting my arms, he said, 'Of course, *anak ko*' (which means "my child"), and with a smile on my face I hugged him tighter and said, 'Thank you, *Amang*' ("Father"). Buffalo also eat young corn, but I let my father give her this treat.

Along the way, I noticed that she was wagging her tail left and right through the grass, sometimes in full circles. This image remained in my mind and still touches me. At first I ignored it, but the tail-wagging went on and on. This gave me the idea to catch her tail every time it touched my back. I had to be careful not to make any sudden movements. I did not want to make Luning-Ning uncomfortable or to startle her, because she might suddenly sidestep, jump, or break into a run, and my father and I would have toppled to the ground because we didn't use a saddle to sit on a buffalo like Westerners do when they ride a horse. So, whenever Luning-Ning's tail touched my back, I tried to catch it, hold on to it for a bit and then let it go. We were playing a game of catch. I had to remain alert because I could not see whether she would swing her tail to the left or the right. We continued our little game as we approached the grassy field.

The next day, I let my father look after Luning-Ning on his own. He had to leave early to join the other farmers in repairing the irrigation dam at the river that flowed into the neighbouring village. Riding on Luning-Ning, it would take him an hour and a half. Repairing dams was a monthly job in normal weather, but after a storm or flooding farmers would do it more often. They used big rocks and large sacks of pebbles, packing them together to trap the water, which irrigated the paddy fields. My father promised that I could have more time with Luning-Ning in the coming days.

So, the next morning before getting ready for school, I ate my breakfast of steamed rice that my mother had cooked with sweet potato leaves that I had picked from the vegetable garden that morning. I dipped the food in a home-made fish sauce and lemon juice. It was delicious. Then I fetched a bucket of water from the pump for my shower. I used a big empty vegetable oil can as a bucket. After my shower, I helped with household chores before beginning the thirty-minute walk to school.

My route took me down a long, winding road. Some portions

of it were just a footpath, and here I would take a shortcut. I didn't like walking along the grassy footpath the whole time, especially in the morning because the dew made my feet wet. However, in the afternoon the grass would be dry and I had to worry about grass snakes. I was very scared of snakes and didn't like the way they looked, how they slithered, their colours or their skin. They gave me goosebumps and I ran as fast as I could whenever I saw one, no matter how small it was. In the afternoon after school, I sometimes walked with my friends, but they took the bus in the morning, whereas I always walked to and from school. My parents could not afford the bus fare. I had time to walk to school; I just needed to leave early.

There was a stream on my shortcut; across the stream was a coconut tree trunk so that people could cross, but nothing to hold on to and it could be slippery when it was wet, so I needed to cross carefully. It was better in the afternoon because it was dry by then. The other children and I were so used to the coconut bridge that sometimes we even ran along it. We liked walking home on that path after school. It was our way of relaxing. Along the way we girls would pick wild guavas and eat them. The boys were normally more interested in looking for spiders. They would collect them and compare to see who had the biggest one, then keep it in a wooden box with a little square section where they put the spider.

My father mostly let me concentrate on my schoolwork during the week, and if he was not around he allowed me to look after Luning-Ning. I was grateful for the trust he had in me.

2

Collecting Wood

My real adventures with Luning-Ning took place at the weekends. This was when we could do fun stuff together. I would teach her to obey commands such as lying down or standing up, walking backwards or forwards, stopping or running. I would also ride her and find nice grass for her to eat. We would be together for hours in the early morning when the grass was fresh, and again in the late afternoon when the sun was not too hot for her.

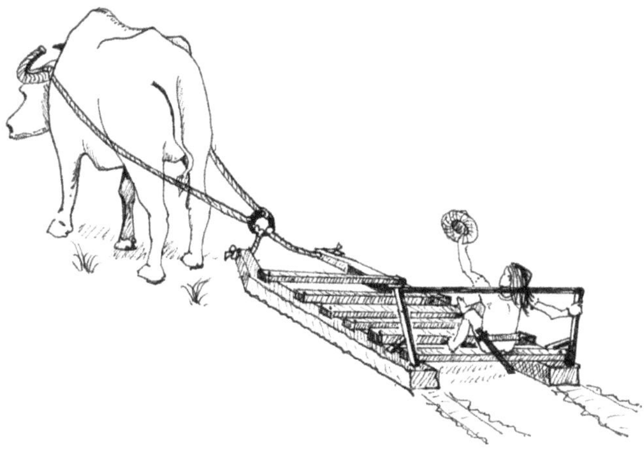

When I was younger, I'd helped my father with chores, but eventually he let me do some of them on my own. I realized that he thought that I was still too young for big jobs like collecting firewood, and I knew I could not do it as efficiently as he could, but I could still do something to help him. My father made a *pasagad* or *pattuki*: a big wooden sledge that we used for collecting wood or anything else that was heavy. We would attach it to Luning-Ning's neck and she would pull it. On most weekends we went to my father's woods and collected the dry fallen branches, or my father would climb trees and cut branches with his machete. I too climbed trees with a machete in its case, which was attached by a string to my waist. We gathered the wood into piles and put it on the *pasagad*, tied it securely and let Luning-Ning pull the load for us. If she was pulling anything heavy I didn't ride on her back because I was afraid the combined load would be too much for her, so I walked home with my father, with Luning-Ning in tow.

When we reached home, we detached Luning-Ning's reins from the *pasagad* and gave her water. She would have eaten while we were collecting the wood, so now we let her have a much-deserved rest. My father and I would unload the pile of wood from the *pasagad* into a storage place where we would cut it into small pieces to use on another day.

3

Collecting Bamboo, and Riding by Myself for the First Time

One weekend, when I had more time to spend with Luning-Ning, my father went out early to cut some bamboo and asked me to take her to meet him. The place where my father grew bamboo wasn't far from our house. Bamboo grows tall, but it is easy to grow. Its young shoots grow very fast, to around six metres or more. At first they have a silky, shiny, smooth green skin, but when they are older they turn brown, yellow and green. The wind blowing through their leaves makes a soothing sound, though when the bamboo sways in the wind it makes a scratchy noise, which I used to think was a bit spooky, especially at night. My father had inherited the land from his parents and, in addition to bamboo, he had planted all sorts of other things there: mandarin, pineapple, pomelo, coconut and tamarind.

Luning-Ning and I had to walk on a gravel road, which was also used by cars and motorbikes. It wasn't too busy, though, so I was pretty sure I could manage her on my own, although I hadn't been alone with her on that road before. So in the morning, after she had eaten her crisp, fresh, crunchy green grass, Luning-Ning and I went to meet my father. For me it was exciting because I loved riding her and this was the first time I was allowed to do so by myself. It was also a bit overwhelming, even though I was confident I could do it. It made me feel like a big girl, and I beamed with pride and gave myself a big hurrah! As I rode towards the field I sang my favourite song, or whistled, and everything around me seemed beautiful and perfect.

When we arrived, my father was sitting with his hat off on the grass in the shade of the bamboo trees. There were three different sizes of tree, and I asked him what they were for. He told me that bamboo had many uses, depending on the age and size of the tree and how it was cut. One size was for making ties, for which the bamboo would be cut into thin pieces, almost like string. These were used instead of the plastic or rope ties that could be bought at the market. Bamboo could also be sliced into pieces one to two inches wide, which could be used to construct the walls of a chicken house. The third size was used to make the coop's flooring.

At the end of each felled tree after the first knuckle, my father made a hole big enough to insert a rope. All three trees were connected to Luning-Ning's special harness and we headed home, towing the trees behind us. Again, I didn't ride on her back, though my father had said I could. As we walked home, I thought about how strong Luning-Ning was and how hard it would have been for us to do this work without her. She was a treasure. My father let me lead and hold Luning-Ning's reins. I walked at her pace and he walked behind us.

When we arrived home and unloaded the bamboo, we let Luning-Ning have a long-awaited rest under her favourite mango tree for the remainder of the day. Our house was surrounded by mango trees and we rested under them when it was hot. Luning-Ning had her own tree, which she loved. She didn't eat mango leaves or the fruit. There was grass under the tree, which was cooler for her to lie on. Mango leaves are thick and bushy, and if you stood under a tree and looked up you wouldn't see any sun. That was why mango trees offered such a great place to cool down when we had scorching sun. So Luning-Ning had cool shade throughout the day until it was time for her to eat again in the afternoon.

The next day was great for Luning-Ning because she didn't need to work, as it was a school day. All she had to do was eat in the morning, sleep through the day, eat again in the afternoon and then sleep through the night under her mango tree.

4

A Picnic in the Mountains with Friends and Family

One weekend in particular was very special, because our family were going into the mountains to have a picnic and a swim. And, of course, we were taking Luning-Ning with us. I was to ride on her together with one of my friends and we would meet our relatives and their buffalo on the way. Some riding in twos, some riding alone. We would all go to the mountains together. Our path to the mountains was ideal for the most part: it had been sunny for a long time and the soil was like powder. It was nice and soft under Luning-Ning's feet, which was important because buffalo don't wear shoes like horses in Western countries.

We left home before sunrise when it was cool, which was good for the buffalo as the hot sun makes them uncomfortable. You just know when buffalo need a break from the sun. They begin to look tired and will stand still with their mouths open, panting and agitated. This happens after between thirty minutes and an hour of being in the sun. It depends on the buffalo and not all of them are the same.

It took us about two hours to get to the mountains. Along

the way, we stopped to collect wild fruits such as avocados, which we would put sugar on and eat as a dessert. We also looked for vegetables like banana flowers, which were so nice when barbecued. We found green leafy vegetables such as river ferns and chilli leaves. Yes, we ate chilli leaves! They taste like spinach. Wild bitter gourds grow like vines and crawl along the ground or climb and become tall grasses. They also grow between corn. We ate their leaves, and their fruit was one of my favourites. Taro grows by the river and is either green or dark red like beetroot. My favourite taro was *alukon*. We ate the fruits and the young leaves, which we normally added to soup. My all-time favourite was moringa. In my opinion, it was the best green vegetable. I could have eaten it every day, and I felt the same about bananas and papayas. We even stopped for a coconut break, which meant that one of us had to climb the coconut tree. It was normally boys or adults who did the climbing, as they were stronger. A girl would never be asked to climb up to get a coconut for a boy, and that is still the culture in the Philippines. While we collected vegetables and fruits for our picnic, Luning-Ning and her buffalo friends had a drink from the nearby stream and nibbled some grass from around the water.

When we arrived at our destination it was so beautiful: the trees; the hanging orchids with their white flowers. Some grew attached to the trees and to other climbing plants, which covered the high cliffs by the river. There were other flowers too, which my parents didn't even know the names of; wild plants that you would not see in anyone's garden. Their leaves twinkled in the sun as the wind moved them. The water was so clean and clear that you could see fish swimming in it. There were a lot of baby fish in the shallows among the shellfish. Some of the shells were long and spiky, and others rounded and smooth. They lived on the rocks and between stones. We caught them by feeling with our hands, or by swimming underwater using my father's home-made goggles. He had spent a long time carving their wooden frame using his little knife; then he had cut out a piece of glass and sliced an old bicycle tyre into string for the elastic. We had to be careful not to step on the shells as it could be painful, though they were not poisonous and we would eat the creatures that lived inside them.

The water's depth was deceptive. You would think it was shallow, but it was actually very deep. There was even a rainbow in the water! Well, we kids created that by accident when we threw a big rock into the water and the ripple afterwards had a rainbow-like effect. I was not sure how it had happened but guessed that it was due to a combination of the sun reflecting off the water, and the surrounding green leaves shining in the sunlight. My relatives and I were so amazed by our rainbow discovery. After that, we spent the morning jumping into the water from the huge rocks that were scattered along the river. Some of them were as big as the stones at Stonehenge, and dark grey in colour.

Luning-Ning and her friends were allowed to remain in the water for as long as they wanted. We swam around them and splashed water on them. They were happy to lie down with just their heads sticking above the water, watching us having fun. They tilted their heads from side to side to get their horns wet and cool down. They were water buffalo, after all!

After our swim, we had a delicious picnic: fish caught by one of the adults using an arrow gun made by my father, together with shellfish and river prawns, which we caught with our hands. You must be patient to catch river prawns in this way. We let the adults catch the big ones, as their claws could nip quite painfully. Everyone helped to collect the fish and it was always fun when the adults and children worked together as a team. Together with the vegetables and fruits we had picked along the way, the fish made the best picnic. Then we returned to the water, and everyone had more fun swimming, diving, jumping, and playing tag using a rock as a base. The boys found a hanging vine root. It was thick and strong, and they climbed a quarter of the way up the cliff, from where they could swing out across the water before plummeting in. Some of them made monkey sounds as they swung. There was a lot of noise and laughter; pure fun for us all.

We had such a wonderful day, but then it was time to go home. We let the buffalo walk slowly and graze on the grass alongside the path. Our journey took longer because they were hungrier than they usually were. The grass was not as crisp as it had been that morning, and it was a bit wilted after being in the sun all day. It hadn't rained for quite a while and the grass desperately needed water. The grass near the stream was better and healthier and there were trees to give the buffalo shade.

We said goodbye to our relatives, who lived on the other side of the hill, and continued our journey home. It would take longer to travel around the hill because our only forms of transport were the buffalo cart and walking. If we wanted to see our neighbours, we always walked. It was easier. It wasn't a smooth path, especially heading uphill, where it was uneven. The path followed the rainwater down to the stream and eventually to the river, where it became a long, deep hole. When it rained it was muddy, so walking was the best way to go anywhere.

When we got home I tied Luning-Ning's reins to her mango tree and asked her if she had had a great time on our picnic adventure. To my surprise, she replied with a long 'Maaaaaaaaaah!' I laughed happily and hugged her. We stayed together for a few minutes. The time I spent with her was the best part of my day. I said goodnight and walked away with a huge grin on my face. I kept what had happened to myself, because I did not think my family would believe me if I told them that I had just had a good conversation with Luning-Ning. I went to bed that night still thinking about it.

5

The River with the Steep Hill

One very, very hot day during harvest season, Luning-Ning was helping us to collect corn using a *Karison*, which is like a two-wheeled trailer made from bamboo and wood. She could not remain in the sun for too long, and when it was time for her to have a break, my father asked me to take her to the river nearby for a drink and a swim.

The path to the river was very steep, so I had to be careful. I did not want Luning-Ning to be injured, which would have been a disaster as we did not have an animal doctor in our village. I think she sensed my worry and concern. She kept stopping, wagging her tail, and making funny head movements as if she was nodding. I realized she was telling me something, so I asked her if she could get down this difficult path to the river, since neither of us had done it before. She moved her back feet to the left and right as if telling me not to be afraid; that we could do it together.

I gave her a signal to go by applying gentle pressure to her sides with my feet. My father did this all the time, so I tried it and it worked. She started walking. I was still terrified, so I kept my legs squeezed tight around her back. It was like walking downstairs, and I felt sure I would slide forwards and land on Luning-Ning's neck. That would be uncomfortable for her and she would shake me off onto the ground in seconds. I would definitely be hurt. Then she gave me a sign, by wagging her tail continuously. It clicked. She wanted me to hold her tail as we descended, so I would not fall off. I caught her tail and asked her if she wanted me to hold on to it, and she nodded her head. That was when I knew we had a secret understanding, a unique connection.

We moved slowly down the path, navigating our way as smoothly as we could. We made it to the bottom and reached the edge of the river. I got off Luning-Ning's back and let her have a well-deserved drink and a swim to cool down. I watched her enjoying the cold, fresh water, a smile on my face as I thought about what had just happened. I was convinced that I had a special connection with her and was beginning to understand her more and more as I discovered more about her. As soon as we'd reached the river she had gulped thirstily at the water, and I had splashed her over and over again. I knew she loved it because she was grinning, showing me her white teeth and tilting her head from side to side. Then she dipped her face into the water as if playing peekaboo; she seemed to be having so much fun. After this, I left Luning-Ning in the water and joined my father to have lunch. Again, I didn't tell him or anyone else about what had happened between Luning-Ning and me.

After lunch, as I walked down to the river to collect Luning-Ning, I was thinking about how amazing it was to have her as my special friend. I undid her rope, which was tied to a big tree root sticking out from the river's edge. Before we headed back up, I splashed water on her face one more time. This time I walked in front of her instead of riding on her back. We walked slowly up to the top, where the surface was flat, then I hopped on her back and rode to join my father and continue our work. I was really just tagging along with him, but he didn't mind and I enjoyed it. But my main reason for helping him was to be with Luning-Ning. I think he had worked this out because he let me be with her and take her to the river on my own. I was very happy to do so whenever she needed a drink and to cool down. Harvest season ran from the middle of March to April for rice, and from April to May for corn. The weather was hot and humid and it hardly rained during those months, so frequent breaks were essential for us and for Luning-Ning. She had been with us for about eight months by this time and I felt comfortable and confident around her.

It was such a long day and we were all pleased when it was time to go home and have a rest. I said goodnight to Luning-Ning and thanked her for all her hard work, and for our wonderful exchange by the river when I'd discovered that we understood each other. I could not wait to learn more about her. She went to lie down on her bed of dried rice straw. I gave her a goodnight pat and left.

6

Luning-Ning Gets Lost for a Day

One evening in October, we left Luning-Ning in the field overnight with some other buffalo owned by my father's friends, and walked home. At that time, we didn't know that there would be a storm that night. The skies were pretty clear when we left her.

When the storm woke me in the middle of the night, I could hear strong wind and heavy rain. In the Philippines the rain was so heavy that it marked the ground. It was pitch black outside; there were no street lights and, since there were a lot of trees around our house, the wind and rain looked stronger than they actually were.

Any typhoon always wrecked or half-wrecked our house. Something would invariably be blown off. If it wasn't the roof, then it would be the wall, or it could be both. Our roof was made of cogon grass, which is about a metre long or more. It was tied together neatly into about ten inches in diameter and then arranged in a compact row along the roof beam and secured with bamboo string. The walls were fashioned from coconut wood cut into long planks two inches thick. We didn't really know when rain or storms would come because we didn't have radio or television to get the forecast. Most people in my village predicted the weather based on the appearance of the sky and the sound of the Pacific Ocean's waves. Although we were far from the sea, we could see it in the distance. My father would tell us to brace ourselves and be prepared in case the house was demolished by the typhoon.

This was Luning-Ning's first storm since she had been with us, so I immediately thought of her and whether she would be all right. I hoped she was not too scared. I could not sleep, and could hardly wait until I could check on her at first light. When it was finally bright enough to go outside, my father and I set off to check on Luning-Ning. As we approached the field, we scouted around but could not see her anywhere. The stump to which my father had tied her was gone. I thought she must have been very scared during the storm. Perhaps she had tried to make her way back home, but had got lost in the dark? Now we didn't know where she was.

We wanted to find her quickly, so my father and I walked in different directions, looking for her. As I walked, I called out her name. Moving through the field, I tried to make buffalo sounds like hers, peering round every tree to see if she was resting against it. I couldn't find her anywhere. I was losing hope, and wondered if my father would find her. I was so worried that I began to cry, screaming her name over and over. I do not remember how far I walked or how long I shouted for her. All that mattered was finding her.

I was some distance from my father when I noticed movement from within a big bush. I ran towards it, crashing through low, spiky bushes and tall grasses with sharp edges that cut and scratched my skin. It stung but I didn't mind. As I got closer to the bush, my feet sank into the swampy grass. When I pulled them free, I left one of my flip-flops behind. I groped through the slimy mud to retrieve it, removed my other flip-flop and held them both in my hand. Barefoot now, I had to walk carefully in case I stepped on something sharp, but luckily there wasn't anything.

And there she was, looking stressed and agitated, but I could also sense her pleasure when she looked up and saw me. I felt a huge wave of relief. Her rope, still attached to the stump, was tangled around the bush. I was so pleased to see her that I hugged her face, and she stood very still. I was glad to smell her special smell, which was like stale beer but warm and comforting. I sensed that she was happy to see me too, as she wagged her tail, took little steps and rubbed her face gently against me. She must have been so scared during the storm that she had run off. I felt so sorry for leaving her on the eve of a storm. I untangled her rope from the bush. As soon as she was free, she came to me and gave me a kiss. Touching her nose to my chest, she let out a long 'Maaaaaaaaaah!' She looked so excited, smiling and nodding at me, and I started to laugh and cry at the same time with happiness, satisfied at finding her. She was all right and we could continue our adventures together.

7

Luning-Ning Has a Baby

Three years passed and the day arrived when Luning-Ning gave birth to her baby.

I remember when my father told me that he was going to mate Luning-Ning with another farmer's buffalo. I didn't go with them as he said that those things were grown-up stuff. Luning-Ning got lucky the first time she was mated.

During her pregnancy she didn't do any work in the rice fields. My father let her rest and I was even more motivated to make sure she had plenty of fresh grass to eat. She would let me rub and feel her tummy, and she seemed to love it. She would stand still and close her eyes, and when I stopped she would open them again and groan, asking me to continue. When I could feel movement in her tummy I got so excited, and yelled so that my father would hear me, but he just replied, 'OK.' I asked him why he wasn't as excited as me. Then he came outside and checked Luning-Ning's tummy too, and he smiled. I knew he was happy too. We had a bet on who could guess the calf's gender. I thought it would be a girl. I felt guilty about riding on Luning-Ning when her tummy was huge, so I walked beside her with one hand on her tummy instead. My father and I were so excited.

Out of respect for her privacy, my father didn't let me help with Luning-Ning while she was in labour. But I was allowed to be near her as soon as she had finished delivering her calf. I could see her giving birth in an empty field near our house, but I was not near enough to really see what was happening. I waited patiently until finally my father waved his hand to invite me to come and see Luning-Ning and her newborn. I was excited to see them. As soon as I got there my father said, with a smile, 'Look, it's a boy,' and I told him, 'Well guessed, Father,' though I wished I had won the bet. My father and I had agreed that if the calf was a boy he would be called Bumaro, which means "young and free".

Though exhausted after giving birth, Luning-Ning was thrilled to be with her new baby. He tried to stand up, but was so wobbly that he kept falling to the ground. Luning-Ning cleaned Bumaro, keeping close to him and inspecting every inch of him.

It was beautiful to watch. I could tell that she was happy to have her son. My father told me that I had another buffalo to look after now, and I was filled with such joy and happiness. I said, 'Father, I am more than happy to look after them,' and he gave me a gentle pat on the shoulder and said, 'That's my good girl.' He smiled, and I grinned cheerfully.

After a few days, Bumaro could walk and run properly and I could tell that he was enjoying running around. Often he was too curious and would run too far from his mum, and with a loud 'Maaaaaaaaaah' Luning-Ning would call him back. Their calls to each other were so lovely. I could not wait until Bumaro was big enough for me to ride. I longed for more exciting adventures in the future with him and Luning-Ning.

8

The Buffalo Celebration Harvest

It was the end of the harvest season and our village was celebrating. The farmers had gathered in the farmers' hall in the middle of the rice field. This was basically an open building with a corrugated-iron roof and a concrete wall around it, and benches for people to sit on when the farmers had their meetings there.

It was a long day, but also one of celebration and fun for the villagers and our buffalo. There were games and competitions, and anyone could participate. Owners raced with their buffalo, and there were awards for the most impressive buffalo, the most masculine male, the most obedient buffalo and the most intelligent. All the award winners were voted for by the farmers, and Luning-Ning received a special award for being the gentlest buffalo and the only one with a broken horn. She and I went to collect her prize, which was a big bunch of freshly cut green grass. I gave it to her straight away and she loved it, gobbling it up quickly. Her munching confirmed how much she enjoyed the grass, and I beamed with pride.

There were a lot of kids there. We went to the same school. A few were my classmates, and there were some older children too. We played together, climbing, rolling down and hiding in a big pile of rice straw, tumbling, jumping, building playhouses, and when we were tired we just lay on the straw. The adults played guitars, sang, drank, laughed and danced. Everyone had a great time. The buffalo were tied to their stumps nearby, watching their humans. Perhaps they were communicating with each other too, as they maaaaaaaaaahed to each other and munched grass. Bumaro did not come to the celebrations; he was too young so he stayed behind. Everyone knew that the day was all about having fun.

9

Buffalo in the Mud

It was the rainy season, which was the time to prepare the paddy fields for planting rice. The paddy fields were always muddy, mucky and a little bit slimy on our bare feet. The mud was very soft and our feet would slide into it. Sometimes we sank right up to our knees. Farmers like my father needed buffalo to help turn the soil using ploughs. Our plough was pulled by Luning-Ning and my father let me have a go with it, but it was too heavy. Still, I liked copying my father and I loved helping him, so he was happy for me to tag along with him.

Bumaro didn't come with us because he had only just been introduced to wearing reins. It was taking a while for him to adjust to them, and my father thought it would be too boring for him to come along only to be tied up nearby and watch Luning-Ning, my father and I do the work. He was too young to work and would need to be properly trained by my father first. For now he was still a baby, but a big baby.

Ploughing was the first step in the preparation of the paddy fields. The next was to smooth and flatten the soil so that it became more like soft mud. My father attached a *balsa*, or flat piece of wood with hooks like big forks in it, to Luning-Ning. She walked through the soil over and over until the *balsa* worked it into soft mud. I loved going to the rice paddy with my father, especially when he was flattening the soil with the *balsa*. I would walk behind him and Luning-Ning, and catch *ararawan*, or field crickets, along the way. I loved catching them with my hands; however, it was not easy, as they could fly, swim, and hide under the mud. They also nipped my fingers with their little claws. It was like an ant bite and not that painful. They hid under the mud when I was about to pick them up, so I needed to be quick and alert. With the passing of every farming season, I became an expert in catching *ararawan*. Sometimes they escaped, and then I would catch them again. I had to be prepared to get muddy. I had a special net basket, and when it was too heavy to carry, I left it at the side of the paddy field. I had to tie up the top bit of the basket so the *ararawan* wouldn't escape, and then I would fill another.

It was quite difficult to run in the mud and I fell over many times. My skin and clothes would be covered with mud, and my father would laugh when he saw me. He called me a muddy, mucky girl, and we both laughed at my appearance. My father also became very muddy, particularly when Luning-Ning splashed him with her tail that was swinging non-stop. I loved catching the field crickets, and would catch as many as I could to take home. I wasn't bothered by the mud and knew I could have a wash when I returned home. Also, I would wash the crickets well and then fry them in oil until they were crunchy and delicious.

At about five in the afternoon it was time to call it a day. Luning-Ning had worked all day, apart from a break when we took our break. It was cloudy and drizzling, so the conditions were perfect for her. After all, she was a water buffalo! We stopped and packed everything away, and I collected my baskets of *ararawan* from the side of the field. My father let me ride Luning-Ning all the way home. Although it wasn't far, it was nice to be on top of her. My father walked by our side. It was sometimes tricky for me to hop onto Luning-Ning's back when we were both so muddy and slippery. I could just about reach her back with my hands. My father clamped his hands together and I used them as a step as he hoisted me up. On our way home we stopped at a nearby stream and washed. Luning-Ning's skin was beautiful, shiny and dark grey once more, and we also washed our muddy feet and hands. My mother wouldn't have liked to see us too dirty when we got home!

Back at home, Luning-Ning would have her long-awaited, delicious, freshly cut green grass for dinner and then settle down for the night. After we had cleaned the rest of the mud from our skin and clothes, my father and I would relax too.

10

Bumaro's Training to Become a Working Buffalo

The farmers in my village valued male buffalo. To them they were comparable to Ferraris. Male calves were trained to become working buffalo when they grew up. It was every farmer's desire to have a male buffalo.

Training a buffalo to work was not always easy. Some could be trained without many problems, but others were harder to train. Bumaro was hard to train. He was young and had never done any farm work, so he could be disobedient while he was learning things for the first time. Young buffalo are very playful and Bumaro could be a troublemaker, wanting to fight with other young buffalo. This was normal and I knew that in time my father would train him to behave and follow straightforward commands, such as stopping when we said '*Hoooo!*' and pulled back on his reins at the same time. When we wanted a buffalo to move while we were riding it we would say '*Hinnnnng!*' and squeeze our legs together. These were the two important commands for communicating with buffalo in my village. Another command was '*Idda!*', which meant "lie down", but we seldom used it. '*Atras!*'

meant "go backwards". Each buffalo learned differently. A farmer knew how long it could take to train one, and had to have a lot of patience. One could not rush teaching farm work to a buffalo, and needed to adjust to the buffalo's ability to learn. It could take weeks or even months.

Before my father started training Bumaro, he took him to the rice field where Luning-Ning worked, so he could see his mother working. Father and I hoped that Bumaro would get the idea of how to do the job just by watching her.

While he was still drinking milk from her, Bumaro was always with Luning-Ning. We never drank any of her milk. Taking milk from our buffalo was not a custom in our village. We used powdered milk imported from America in our coffee and for our babies. It did not need to be kept in the fridge. We also drank herbal teas like ginger, lime and lemongrass, which did not need fresh milk. I am sure buffalo milk would have tasted delicious, but we left it for the calves.

When Bumaro began his training, my father tried to put the *sangol* onto his neck. A *sangol* is a piece of wood designed to fit and curve around the back of a buffalo's neck. Both ends are attached to a rope to pull a plough or cart. When the *sangol* was put on him, Bumaro jumped as if he wanted to shake it off. The *sangol* slipped from his neck when he moved his head. He could not stay still. Looking back, I believe it was because the *sangol* made him feel weird. He probably felt as if he was being strangled, and the wood may have been hard on his young skin. He ran when he tried to plough the paddy fields for the first time. So much starting and stopping. On one occasion I noticed my father's frustration, but he just took off his hat, scratched his head, took a deep breath and started again.

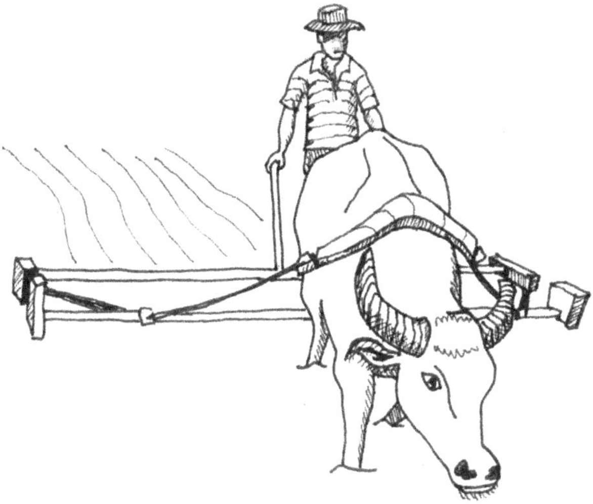

My father trained Bumaro several times a day, but was careful not to overdo it. He was a very patient and calm man, so I think he knew that eventually Bumaro would get it right. He said it was more difficult to train male buffalo. They were more likely than females to be hot-headed and tough. My father said that Bumaro was a *Toro,* which meant he would be a strong, masculine buffalo when he was fully grown. This also meant that it was harder to train him. My father wanted to get it right because a *Toro* that was properly trained was a treasure, but one that was improperly trained was a waste and would be put up for sale. A well-trained *Toro* was strong and able to work all day, although their perfect working environment was still when it was raining and cool.

After Bumaro's training, my father would ask me to remain with him while my father continued to work with Luning-Ning. So, I would take Bumaro for a walk and to eat some grass. I was still not allowed to ride on his back. It was a bit dangerous, as Bumaro needed more training in order to become used to all the tasks that my father was teaching him. His skin was a similar colour to Luning-Ning's. He was very playful when he was with me; he would run around like crazy, sometimes without any reason. I sensed that it was part of him growing up. He would approach me quite closely, look at me curiously and smell me – just look at me and barely touch me with his wet nose. I stroked his head and hugged his face and he stood quietly. Then I would pull up some grass to feed him. He loved it. I would watch him chew and know that we were building a special connection and would one day be best friends and start a new adventure together.

After a few weeks of being trained by my father and me, Bumaro became very good at every type of farm work, particularly ploughing, or pulling the cart filled with wood or sacks of rice or fertilizer. He was basically our main transport. Eventually, Luning-Ning would get older and retire from farm work, which was why my father tried so hard to train Bumaro to take over. We expected Luning-Ning to have her much-deserved retirement then, enjoying her life and just being my companion and a mother to Bumaro.

11

The Last Days of Luning-Ning

With the passing of the farming season, Luning-Ning and Bumaro had time to be together without working in the fields every day. For about two months, they were able to rest, with some odd work here and there, but nothing major. They spent the nights in the fenced-in grassy fields near our house. This allowed them some freedom from wearing their reins or being tied to a nearby tamarind tree. I was happy that they were able to relax, and felt that they deserved this time together. From a distance I watched them eating grass side by side. Sometimes they would look at each other and Bumaro would nudge his mother playfully with his head. Luning-Ning would give a loud 'Maaaaaaaaaah!', and Bumaro would say 'Maaaaaaaaaah!' back to her, and I felt that was love.

One morning when my father went to check on them, he could not believe what he saw. Luning-Ning was just lying on the ground, still and lifeless, and Bumaro seemed agitated and concerned. He was running around maaaaaaaaaahing, and you could tell from his voice that he was crying. My father could not do anything. It was too late to save Luning-Ning. My father thought that, while grazing overnight, she might have eaten a *samrid*: a small, hairy black caterpillar. The *samrid* is extremely poisonous and can kill a buffalo within just minutes.

We were all very sad to see what had happened to Luning-Ning. I missed her terribly – our adventures together, the happy moments we had shared, and how amazing she was. I loved having her in my life. She was my best friend, and I hoped that she had felt the same way about me. She was such a joy to have around. I could always rely on her to do things with me. She always came to the rescue, and she never complained. Our long walks together have a special place in my memory and in my heart. She was not so much my pet, but my friend, my companion. I saw Luning-Ning's spirit in baby Bumaro, and I felt blessed to have been a part of both of their lives.

Epilogue

Luning-Ning was my feet when I was tired of walking, my wobbly ladder when I needed to pick jackfruit from the tree, or when I tried to reach a banana flower that was too high. Without her I could not have carried the sacks of wild guavas that I picked at the farm. She was so gentle. I could stand on top of her back and she would stay very still. I could also lie on top of her and she would keep me safe, knowing that I was resting. I enjoyed our times together under her tree, when she would lie down in the grass and I would use her neck as a pillow. We had a powerful connection and we understood one another.

The End

CPSIA information can be obtained
at www.ICGtesting.com
Printed in the USA
BVHW071454091122
651532BV00008B/228

9 781800 422179